and the

SCHOOL HULLABALOO

For Pandora
J.S.

For Mum and Dad
C.E.

Reading Consultant: Prue Goodwin, Lecturer in literacy and children's books

ORCHARD BOOKS
338 Euston Road, London NW1 3BH
Orchard Books Australia
Level 17/207 Kent Street, Sydney, NSW 2000

First published in 2012
First paperback publication in 2013

ISBN 978 1 40831 329 9 (hardback)
ISBN 978 1 40831 337 4 (paperback)

A CIP catalogue record for this book is available from the British Library.

1 3 5 7 9 10 8 6 4 2 (hardback)
1 3 5 7 9 10 8 6 4 2 (paperback)

Printed in China

Orchard Books is a division of Hachette Children's Books,
an Hachette UK company.
www.hachette.co.uk

and the
SCHOOL HULLABALOO

Justine Smith • Clare Elsom

ORCHARD

Zak Zoo lives at Number One, Africa Avenue.
His mum and dad are away on
safari, so his animal family is looking
after him. Sometimes things get a little . . .

. . . *WILD!*

Emily

Pam

Mum

Dad

Zak

Nanny
Hilda

Bob

Petul

Charlie

Mia (Zak's best friend)

Ping

On Monday morning, Zak Zoo woke up early. He jumped out of bed and went to wake his animal family.

Zak's family liked to sleep in funny places. Emily slept in the wardrobe, and Pam slept in the sock drawer.

Bob liked to sleep on the radiator
where it was warm.
"Wake up!" roared Zak, and
everyone woke up at once.

Zak loved the funny breakfasts that Nanny Hilda made. Today, she had cooked flamingo eggs with crispy ants. "Yum!" said Zak.

At Zak's house, meals were very messy and VERY noisy!
"I have to go to school now!" roared Zak, so that everyone heard.

When Zak picked up his school bag, it felt heavy. Ping was hiding inside! "Sorry, Ping," said Zak. "You can't come. Animals don't go to school." Ping crawled out of the bag.

Outside, Zak climbed onto Emily's back. He gave her his bag, and they set off for school.

Zak went over to Mia's house. He didn't notice that some of his animal family were following him!
Zak gave Mia a lift to school.

At the gates, Zak and Mia climbed down from Emily and went in to school. They didn't see Emily, Bob and Pam going in too!

Zak had a new teacher that day,
and her name was Miss Natter.
"Tell me something about you,"
she said.
Zak couldn't think of anything to say.
"Never mind," said Miss Natter.

Just then, Tamsin crawled out of
Zak's lunchbox.

"It's a spider!" screamed Miss Natter.

"Yes," said Zak. "I like tarantulas.
That's something about me!"

Hello, I'm a
tarantula!

Miss Natter began to teach spellings, so
Zak put Tamsin on the floor. Then Petul(
padded in with a letter on her spikes.
Miss Natter frowned, but Zak smiled.
"P is for porcupine," he said. "And post."

potato
purple
paint

Miss Natter let Zak read his letter
to the class.

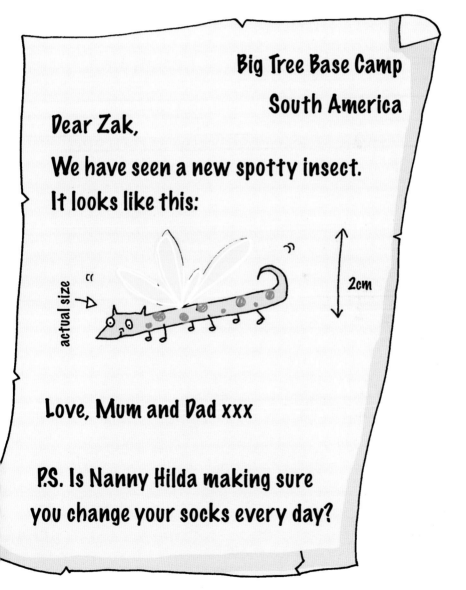

Big Tree Base Camp
South America

Dear Zak,

We have seen a new spotty insect.
It looks like this:

actual size

2cm

Love, Mum and Dad xxx

P.S. Is Nanny Hilda making sure
you change your socks every day?

"Reading books out, please,"
said Miss Natter, when Zak
had finished.

Zak's friend Dora opened her
desk to get her book out.

"It's a ssssssnake!" she screamed.

Everyone jumped onto their chairs.

"Is that really a snake?" cried

Miss Natter.

"Yes," said Zak. "Pam is a python."

Pam gave Zak a hug.

Miss Natter was exhausted. "I must
sit down," she said.
But suddenly, Mia saw Bob. He was
on Miss Natter's chair.

"No!" said Mia. She dived to get Bob.
But she got Miss Natter instead.

Miss Natter's chair wobbled and
she fell on the floor. Bob flew up . . .
and down, into Miss Natter's lap.

"Bob!" said Zak. "What a surprise!"

"Hello, Bob," said Mia.

Bob gave Mia a hug.

Miss Natter jumped onto her desk!

Hello, I'm an iguana!

As she did so, Miss Natter's desk wobbled and some test-tubes fell over. *BANG!* There was a big puff of smoke. "Fire! Fire!" screamed Miss Natter.

potato
purple
paint

BRRRING! The fire alarm went off. Suddenly Emily appeared at the window. She put her trunk in the sink and squirted the fire with water.

Emily sprayed the whole class to make
sure they were safe.

Everyone was dripping wet!

Miss Natter looked at Zak.

Then she looked at Emily.

"This is Emily. She's an elephant," said Zak.

"She's not just an elephant," said
Miss Natter. "She's a hero! She
saved us!"
Everyone clapped. Miss Natter gave
Emily a medal.

After school, Mia came to tea.

"Yum!" said Zak. "I love roast maggots with grilled grasshopper!"

"It's very tasty," said Mia politely.

Then she gave her plate to Charlie.

After tea, Mia went home and Zak sat down to do his homework.
Everyone helped.

The homework was to write a letter.
"I know what I'll write!" said Zak.

Dear Mum and Dad,

I had a good day at school.
It went with a bang. We
also had some visitors!
Love, Zak xxx

P.S. Don't worry,
I changed my socks
last week.

Written by Justine Smith • Illustrated by Clare Elsom

Zak Zoo and the School Hullabaloo   978 1 40831 329 9

Zak Zoo and the Peculiar Parcel   978 1 40831 330 5

Zak Zoo and the Seaside SOS   978 1 40831 331 2

Zak Zoo and the Unusual Yak   978 1 40831 332 9

Zak Zoo and the Hectic House   978 1 40831 333 6

Zak Zoo and the Baffled Burglar   978 1 40831 334 3

Zak Zoo and the TV Crew   978 1 40831 335 0

Zak Zoo and the Birthday Bang   978 1 40831 336 7

All priced at £8.99

Orchard Books are available from all good bookshops,
or can be ordered from our website: www.orchardbooks.co.uk,
or telephone 01235 827702, or fax 01235 827703.

Prices and availability are subject to change.

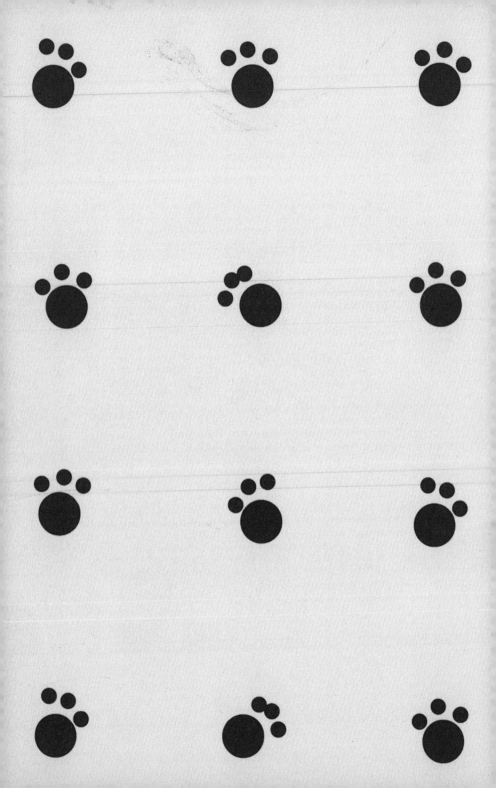